Copyright © 2009 Jenny Alexander
Illustrations copyright © 2009 Mark Oliver
Reading consultant: Andrew Burrell, MA, PhD

First published in Great Britain in 2009
by Hodder Children's Books

The right of Jenny Alexander and Mark Oliver to be identified as the Author
and Illustrator of the Work has been asserted by them in accordance with
the Copyright, Designs and Patents Act 1988.

1

A Catalogue record for this book is available
from the British Library

ISBN 978 0 340 98145 0 (HB)
ISBN 978 0 340 98151 1 (PB)

Typeset by
Tony Fleetwood

Printed and bound in Great Britain by
Clays Ltd St Ives plc, Bungay, Suffolk

The paper and board used in this book are natural recyclable products
made from wood grown in sustainable forests.

Hodder Children's Books
a division of Hachette Children's Books
338 Euston Road, London NW1 3BH
An Hachette UK company
www.hachette.co.uk

CAR-MAD JACK
The Speedy Sports Car

Written by
JENNY ALEXANDER

Illustrated by
MARK OLIVER

Hodder Children's Books

A division of Hachette Children's Books

· CHAPTER 1 ·

Jack Davy was mad about cars. He had two hundred and forty seven toy cars. He had a road map as big as his bedroom floor and a multi-storey garage. He had a remote control jeep that he played with in the garden.

Jack's favourite film was *Cars*. He had seen it seven times. His favourite computer game was *Super Rally Racer* and his favourite book was *Fifty Fascinating Facts about Cars*.

At Christmas time, his letter to Santa always looked like this:

'Dear Santa, Please could you bring me some new cars, car pictures, car books, car films and car games. Thank you.

From Jack.'

Jack's dad and Uncle Archie ran the car supermarket on the edge of town. Every Saturday, Jack's mum dropped him off there for a couple of hours while she went shopping. It was the best day of the week!

Sometimes he went out with his uncle on the transporter to pick up a new car. Sometimes he helped Mrs Merridew in the office, or made a new poster to pin up on the screen beside Dad's desk in the showroom. Dad had put a sign along the top that said 'Jack's Wall of Cars' and the customers always looked at it.

Sometimes he had to help his big cousin Clark to clean and polish the cars. He didn't like Clark but nobody seemed to notice. They all said, 'Clark will be coming in for an hour today – won't that be nice?' As nice as poison pie, thought Jack. But at least it didn't happen very often.

One Saturday, when Jack arrived, his dad had cleared a big space at the front of the showroom, ready for a new car. He was so excited he could hardly keep still.

'Wait until you see it, Jack!' he said. 'We've never had such a fancy car in here before.'

'What sort of car is it?' asked Jack.

Just then, the car transporter pulled up outside the showroom and Uncle Archie jumped down from the driver's seat. Jack and his dad ran out to see the new car. It was a red Ferrari.

'Wow!' cried Jack.

He had never seen a Ferrari before.

Uncle Archie backed it off the transporter and drove it very slowly into the showroom. They all walked around it, admiring the shiny red paint-work, the prancing horse badge and the gleaming silver star-shapes in the wheels.

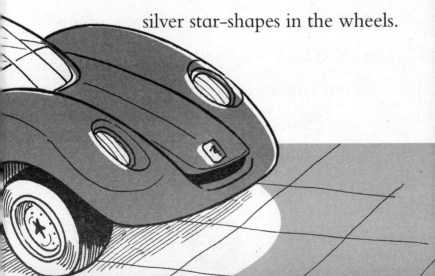

'It looks like a racing car,' Jack said.

'That's because it *is* like a racing car,' said Dad. 'Ferrari started out making racing cars and then used the same methods to make their road cars.'

'This little beauty can do a cool two hundred miles an hour,' added Uncle Archie.

They stood there talking about the new Ferrari for fifteen minutes, until Uncle Archie had to go and pick up another car. Then Jack and Dad got some dusters and gave the gleaming red paintwork an extra polish.

'What kind of person would drive a car like this, Dad?' said Jack.

'Someone with loads of money!' Dad joked. 'A famous footballer, maybe.'

'He could get to matches really quickly in it, couldn't he?' Jack said. 'He could go on the motorway and be anywhere in the country by dinner-time!'

Dad laughed. 'So long as the police didn't catch him,' he said. 'You're only supposed to do seventy miles an hour on the motorways.'

'But they wouldn't,' Jack said. 'Nobody could catch you in this!'

Dad grinned and nodded.

'Well, I'd love to stay here gazing at it all day, but I'd better go and do the paperwork,' he said. He asked Jack if he would like to come and make a Ferrari poster for his famous Wall of Cars.

'Can I sit in it first?' Jack asked.

Dad always let him sit in the new cars while he sorted out the paperwork, but this time he scratched his chin.

'I don't know, Jack. This is a very special car.'

'I won't do anything,' Jack pleaded. 'I know the rules.'

The rules were:

No feet on seats, no food or sweets.

No switches or buttons or brakes.

Jack didn't mind the rules at all. He didn't want to eat in the cars – he wanted to have adventures! He didn't want to put his feet on the seats – why would he? As for messing around with the switches and buttons, most of them didn't work anyway unless the engine was running.

He didn't want to touch the handbrake

either. Imagine! You could find yourself sliding out of control, smashing through the showroom window and finishing up on the forecourt! Pretend games were much better.

'All right then,' Dad said. He opened the driver's door, and Jack got in.

'Drive safely!' said Dad, closing the car door after him.

· CHAPTER 2 ·

Jack put his hands on the steering-wheel and sat there, taking everything in. The seats were very low, covered in the same soft light brown leather as the steering-wheel. Between the seats there was a bank of buttons and dials. Looking through the windscreen, he could see the long red bonnet gleaming in front of him.

The prancing horse in the middle of the steering-wheel seemed to be saying to him, 'Come on, Jack – let's go racing!

What are we waiting for?'

Jack imagined he was Jack Davy, world-famous football striker. He had to get to Birmingham by lunch-time for the quarter-final. He started up his Ferrari. The engine purred. It was the purr of a tiger, not a pussy-cat. It sent a thrill of excitement through him.

Jack drove carefully out on to the forecourt. He couldn't wait to get on to the road. But the entrance was completely blocked by newspaper reporters and fans. 'Oh, no!' thought Jack. 'They must have heard that Jack Davy the football superstar was picking up his car today.'

He had to drive very slowly through the crowd. They didn't want to move out

16

of the way. Cameras flashed. Reporters shouted questions. They held out their microphones for him to reply.

'Is it true you're going out with Kimberley from The Kittenz, Jack?'

'Did you really have a bust-up with the team coach?'

'How are you feeling about the big match today?'

Fans wearing the team strip waved autograph books at him and tried to get

pictures of him with their mobile phones. It was great having lots of fans but Jack kept his windows tightly shut because otherwise they would reach in and grab him or even try to get into the car.

He waved and smiled and kept driving through, forcing them to move. As the crowd got thinner, he was able to speed up a bit. Finally, he left the crowd behind.

The road out of town was busy and he had to keep stopping at traffic lights and crossings. Whenever he stopped, people spotted him and shouted.

'Hey! There's Jack Davy,

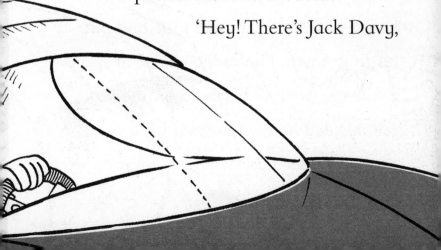

the famous footballer!'

They ran up and tapped on the windows. They shouted, 'Go, Jack!' He smiled and nodded. He gave them a thumbs-up. But all he really wanted was to get away from the people and on to the motorway.

At last, Jack saw the big blue motorway signs up ahead. He pulled over to put the roof down.

'Yes!' he thought. 'Now let's see what this fast Ferrari can do.'

As soon as he was on the motorway, he swept into the outside lane and put his foot down. The sudden burst of speed made the back of his head hit the seat. He decided he had better not try to go at full speed until he had got used to

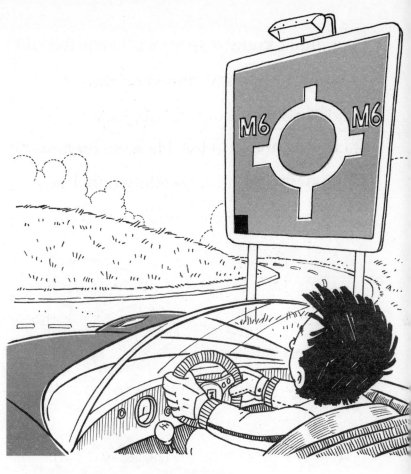

driving such a powerful car.

He slowed down a bit. He was still going faster than the other cars. In every car he passed, people looked and pointed. At this speed, they couldn't tell who was driving so they didn't know it was Jack Davy, famous footballer. They just loved the car. The car was the star.

He was about to put his foot down again when he heard a sound that made his

heart sink. It was a police siren. He saw the flashing blue lights in his rear-view mirror as the police car came up behind him. He saw the policemen signalling at him to pull over.

The prancing horse on the steering wheel seemed to say, 'Put your foot down! Leave the boys in blue behind! They'll never be able to catch up with you!' But he couldn't do it. Partly, he thought, 'The police are there to protect us and keep us safe, so we can't just ignore them.' Partly, he thought, 'They might not be able to catch me right here on the road but they've got my number. That means they'll be able to get my details from the police computer and track me down later.'

He slowed down and stopped on the hard shoulder. The police car pulled over in front. Two policemen got out, put on their hats and walked back towards the car. He opened the window to talk to them.

'Do you know what speed you were

doing, Sir?' one of the policemen asked. He had a bushy grey moustache and eyebrows, and tufts of hair coming out of his ears. Jack shook his head. The other policeman told him, 'Eighty-eight miles an hour.'

'That's eighteen miles an hour faster than the speed limit for this road,' said the hairy policeman. He took his clipboard out from under his arm and felt in his pocket for a pen. Jack noticed that the backs of his hands were hairy too.

'I'm going to have to give you a speeding ticket,' he said.

'But I'm Jack Davy, the famous footballer,' Jack protested. 'I was only speeding because I've got to be in Birmingham by lunch-time for the quarter final.'

'I don't care if you're Donald the famous duck,' said the hairy policeman, writing something down. 'Just because you're famous doesn't mean you can go breaking the law. Now show me your driving licence please.'

While he was checking Jack's driving licence, the other policeman bent down and peered in the window. He whistled through his teeth.

'Wow!' he said. 'You really are Jack Davy! Can I have your autograph?'

The hairy policeman pulled him out of the way.

'For heaven's sake, Smith, he's got a big enough head already.'

'And a big enough car,' said PC Smith, standing back to admire the fabulous Ferrari.

The hairy policeman finished writing out the speeding ticket. 'I think this is a silly car,' he said. 'What's the point of having a car that can do two hundred miles an hour when the fastest you're allowed to go is seventy?'

'Now, Mr Davy, here is your speeding

ticket. If you don't want to get any more, I suggest you stick to the limit from now on.'

'But how am I going to get to Birmingham in time for the match?"

The hairy policeman wasn't listening. He was marching PC Smith back to the police car.

'Blooming celebrities in their fast flashy cars,' he muttered. 'Who do they think they are?'

· CHAPTER 3 ·

'Dad?' said Jack.

Jack was kneeling at the low table between the two sofas in the reception area, trying to draw the red Ferrari. He couldn't seem to get the shape right.

'Yes, Jack?'

Dad was tidying his desk, though it already looked tidy enough to Jack.

'What's the point in having a car that can do two hundred miles an hour if you're only actually allowed to go at seventy?'

'Hmm ...' Dad stopped tidying and thought about it. 'That's a good question,' he said. 'I mean, you wouldn't normally go over the limit or you'd end up losing your driving licence.' They looked at each other, stumped.

'I suppose it's just the idea that's exciting,' Dad said at last. 'It must feel amazing just to know you're driving one of the fastest cars in the world.'

Jack remembered how he had felt when he first got in behind the wheel and the prancing horse seemed to say, 'Let's go racing!'

'Or maybe,' Dad went on, 'the point is that it's simply beautiful. I mean, just look at it!' He gazed across at the red Ferrari, sighing a happy sigh.

Jack rubbed out what he had done and tried again. Dad was right – it was a beautiful car, and he really wanted to get the shape right. When a smart-looking couple came over and started talking to Dad, Jack glanced up and went straight back to his drawing.

'We're interested in the four-by-four

you've got parked on the forecourt,' the man said.

'A very good choice,' said Dad. 'The Range Rover is a lovely vehicle. It's practical and powerful.'

He got the keys and took the couple outside to have a proper look.

Jack remembered the great adventure he had had in that car. It had involved going off-road on Dartmoor. Dad told him four-by-fours were built for driving in wild places, though most people who bought them usually didn't get any further than the ring-road.

Jack's picture was starting to look good. He went over the pencil outline with a black felt-tip pen. Then he got out his colouring pencils. He had his own drawer in Dad's desk with all the things he needed for making posters. He chose the brightest red and started colouring in.

Colouring was the best part and Jack knew he was good at it. You could hardly see the pencil-marks. He filled in the long sleek bonnet, taking his time. He filled in the doors. When Mrs Merridew brought him some orange juice and a slice of home-made chocolate cake, he said thank you and went right on colouring.

As he was colouring in the the last bit of red body-work, he heard someone behind him.

'Look, Dad,' he said, sitting back. 'I've nearly finished.'

He looked round. It wasn't Dad. It was Clark.

'What's that supposed to be?' Clark said. 'It looks like something Fat Brian sat on!'

Fat Brian was one of the mechanics who helped Uncle Archie fix the cars in the workshop. He wasn't really fat, just big and brawny. Clark had nasty nicknames for everyone, even his own dad. He called Jack

'Flapjack', as in 'Don't get in a flap, Jack', which he was fond of saying whenever he had managed to wind Jack up.

Jack wished he would go away. He loved his Saturdays at the car supermarket but when Clark was there he spoiled everything. Clark didn't even like cars. He only came to the car supermarket to earn some pocket money. And he did such a rubbish job of washing and polishing the cars that sometimes Uncle Archie had to do them again after he'd gone home. Jack was sure that if Clark had not been Uncle Archie's son he'd have got the sack months ago.

'Oh-oh, here comes the Slippery Suit,' Clark hissed under his breath, as Jack's

Dad came back into the showroom. 'I'm out of here!'

Jack felt like a balloon that someone had let the air out of. He had been so pleased with his drawing, but now he thought it looked stupid. When his dad leaned over to have a look at it, he wished he could run away and hide.

'That's brilliant!'
Dad said.

He picked up the picture and held it out in front of him. Jack frowned. 'No it isn't,' he said. 'It looks like something Brian sat on.'

Dad gave Jack a puzzled look. 'What an odd thing to say. I think it looks just like a red Ferrari. You've got a real talent, Jack.'

'Clark said—'

Dad didn't let him finish his sentence.

'He's a joker, that Clark!' he chuckled. 'He was just teasing you. He didn't mean it.'

Clark was a joker all right. He loved his little jokes. He found nothing funnier than splashing Jack accidentally-on-purpose when they were cleaning cars, or dropping his bucket on Jack's foot. He once stuck Jack's pencils together with super-glue – ha,

ha! He once pulled out Jack's chair just as
he was about to sit on it.

Dad put the picture back on the table.
'I'm pretty sure that couple will buy the
Range Rover,' he said, looking out the
window. They were walking around it,
opening and shutting the doors. They were

getting in and out. They were standing back and then moving up close to rub an imaginary spot on the paintwork. They were doing all the things customers always did when they knew they were going to buy but hadn't quite got used to the idea.

'I'll get the forms ready while you finish your picture,' said Dad.

But Jack didn't want to do his picture any more. He didn't want to go out into

the yard, either, because Clark was out there washing a black Ford Ka that had just come in.

'Can I sit in the Ferrari again?' he said.

Dad smiled and squeezed his shoulder. 'Of course you can,' he said. 'With any luck, it will inspire you to finish that wonderful poster.'

· CHAPTER 4 ·

The prancing horse on the steering-wheel said, 'Come on Jack! What are we waiting for? Let's go racing!'

But Jack sighed. 'We'd only get stopped by the police again,' he said.

'Pah!' said the prancing horse. 'We won't get stopped if we do a proper race. A car like this doesn't need a footballer and a boring old motorway. It needs a racing driver and a high-speed track.'

Jack put his hands on the steering wheel.

He imagined he was Lightning Jack Davy, the famous racing driver, winner of five Grand Prix races. Every time he won, the TV reporters came crowding around to get video footage of him shaking the champagne bottle and showering everyone with fizz.

But during a race no one could get near him – no reporters, no fans, no police. The crowds had to stay at a safe distance behind the barriers. The empty race track

was waiting for him. He drove out on to it
to do his warm-up lap, parading proudly
in front of the crowds. He zig-zagged to
warm up and clean off the tyres, and then
moved into position for the start.

Down went the green flag. The tiger's
purr burst into a mighty roar as Lightning
Jack shot off like a rocket. He hammered
down the straight and took the first bend
with a squeal of tyres, not wanting to lose
too much speed. But after the bend, all
the cars were still in a pack. He hadn't
managed to push ahead.

Lightning Jack hammered on. The car
shook as the needle rose towards maximum
speed. The sunlight flashed off the metal
cars on either side. The noise of the engines
was deafening. A silver Porsche just in front

of him blew a tyre, lost control and skidded sideways into the barriers.

He was coming up to a big S-shaped bend – what was the word for that? Oh, yes – a chicane! He swerved to the left, hardly slowing down, holding his nerve. He swerved to the right. Two cars just behind him clipped each other and skittered away across the track in a storm of sparks and a screech of tyres.

Coming out of the chicane, Jack found himself at the front of the pack. Could he hold the lead? There was a deadly hairpin bend coming up. He would have to drop his speed or lose control, but if he didn't keep his speed he would lose his place at the front of the pack.

Clouds of dust flew up as Lightning Jack hit the hairpin bend. He could hear the other cars but he couldn't see them. He gripped the steering-wheel so hard that his knuckles hurt as he tried to stay on the track.

Straightening up after the bend he saw he was still winning! A rush of happiness swept through him as he went into the final circuit.

It didn't last. Moments later, Jack saw out of the corner of his eye a black car catching

47

up with him. It drove alongside. They were neck and neck. Jack had his foot on the floor, but he still couldn't shake the other car. Glancing sideways, he caught a split-second glimpse of the driver. He knew that face!

It was Crasher Clark – so-called because everyone knew he was the dirtiest driver in the business. The last time the two of them had been in a race together, Crasher Clark had driven Lightning Jack into the barriers and his car had exploded in a ball of flame.

Lightning Jack had never beaten Crasher Clark before. He felt like giving up. What was the point in trying? He would only end up getting hurt.

'What's going on?' yelled the prancing horse on the steering wheel. 'We're losing him!'

The Crasher was pulling ahead. Too late, Jack realised that he shouldn't have let that happen. Now Crasher Clark had a chance to clip the front corner of the Ferrari, sending it into a skid.

Lightning Jack didn't get into a flap. Using all his skill and courage, he kept control of his car and managed not to go into a spin. As he straightened up, he suddenly found he wasn't scared any more – he was angry.

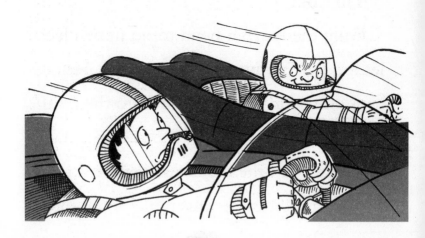

'I'll get you, Crasher Clark!' he thought.

They were coming up to the chicane again. They swerved to the left. Swerved to the right. They came into the straight, just the two of them now, way out in front, battling it out for first place.

Bang! Crasher Clark hit the side of his car, but this time he got it wrong. Instead of Jack going into a skid, he was the one who had to struggle to keep control. In those few seconds, Lightning Jack edged out in front.

Only the hairpin bend to go now. 'Please let me win!' prayed Lightning Jack. He took the bend well and shot into the final straight.

Down went the black-and-white flag as he roared across the finish line! Up jumped the crowds, cheering and waving their arms. The fabulous Ferrari shuddered as it slowed down and finally came to a stop.

'Now that's what I call a race!' said the prancing horse.

· CHAPTER 5 ·

The smart young couple were sitting
opposite Dad discussing deals across
his desk. Jack didn't understand about
nought per cent loans and all the other
complicated things Dad had to go through
when he made a sale. He sat down quietly
at the small table and looked at his Ferrari
poster, happy to let their money-talk wash
over him.

What did Clark know about cars? He
didn't even like them! He wouldn't know

a Ferrari from a Fiat, so who was he to judge whether Jack's picture looked like one?

'I was silly, listening to Clark,' thought Jack, picking up the black pencil to colour in the tyres.

By the time he had finished his poster, the smart couple were filling in forms. Dad was looking very pleased with himself. He loved it when he made a sale. Suddenly the phone on the corner of his desk rang. He frowned at it, not picking it up. It stopped ringing, then started again. All of them were looking at it now. Jack's dad shrugged and answered it.

'Yes?' he said. 'Hmm ... I see ... can I phone you back?'

The answer must have been no, because

he put his hand over the phone and mouthed, 'Would you excuse me, please? I've really got to take this.' The smart couple said it was quite OK.

While they were waiting for Jack's dad to come off the phone, they sat back

and looked around.

'What's that you've been drawing?' the woman asked Jack.

He showed her his new poster.

'It's that one over there,' he said, pointing at the red Ferrari.

'You've done a great job,' she remarked. 'Your picture looks just like it.'

The man was standing up, looking at Jack's Wall of Cars. He said, 'Do you do a poster for every car?'

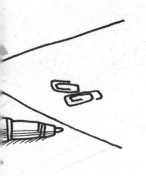

Jack shook his head. 'No. Just the ones I like.'

He always wrote a comment about the car under the picture. Dad said it had to be something good because the idea of putting up posters was to sell cars, not put people off. So if he couldn't think of anything good to say, he didn't make a poster.

'Hey!' the man exclaimed. 'Here's our Range Rover Discovery, Roselle!'

She stood up to take a closer look.

At the bottom of the drawing Jack had written:

For Sale – Silver Range Rover.
It's a rugged 4 by 4.
Ekselent for driving across Dartmoor,
a long way from any roads.
You could also use it to take
your children to playgroup.

While they were reading the poster, Clark came into the showroom on his way to Mrs Merridew's office. He spread the fingers of one hand wide in a secret signal to Jack as he came in. It meant, 'I'm getting five whole pounds for washing that Ka! Too bad you're small and useless and don't get paid for anything around here.'

'All right, Flapjack?' he said out loud, as

he walked past. He told the smart couple,
'That's my cousin. I call him Flapjack
because he's so sweet!'

'Fetch the sick bucket,' thought Jack.
Just then, his dad came off the phone.

'Now, where were we?' he asked the young couple.

The man said, 'We've been admiring Jack's Wall of Cars. It's most impressive.'

Jack's dad nodded and smiled. 'I think he sells more cars than me,' he said.

'What will happen to our Range Rover poster now that we've bought the car?' said the man.

'Would it be possible to buy it?' the woman asked.

'You'd better ask Jack,' said Dad.

Now Jack was having some money-talk! He didn't know what to say. Luckily the man asked straight out, 'Would you take ten pounds for it?' Ten pounds!

Jack grinned and nodded.

'We'll frame it and put it on the nursery

wall for this little one when he arrives,' said the woman, stroking her tummy, which Jack suddenly noticed was very big and round.

Dad gave the couple the keys to their new car and they shook his hand. Jack

gave them the Range Rover poster and they shook his hand too. As they were leaving, Clark came out of the back office, waving his five-pound note in the air. He stopped when he saw Jack grinning up at his dad with a ten-pound note in his hands.

'What's going on?' Clark asked – Dad, not Jack. 'Where did he get all that money from?'

'It seems some people love Jack's pictures, even if other people think they look like something Brian sat on!' Dad said, winking at Jack.

Clark stomped off in a mood.

'Right!' Dad said, after he had gone. 'Pass me that

Ferrari – we've got a gap to fill!'

He pinned the new poster up on Jack's
Wall of Cars. They stood there looking
at it.

It looks like a racing car and it can go at two hundred miles an hour. You mustn't go above seventy or the police will give you a speeding ticket, but it's a great feeling to know that you could. This car is magic!

Jack

'Ah, yes,' sighed Dad, happily. 'What a car!'

Jack nodded. It really was a magic car, he thought. Before it had come, he had never beaten Clark at anything, even in his dreams. In that fast Ferrari, he had dared to dream of beating Clark and then . . . He put the crisp ten-pound note in his pocket.

Then his dream had come true.

**Look out for more of
Car-mad Jack's adventures
in the following books:**

**The Versatile Van
The Motorbike in the Mountains
The Marvellous Minibus
The Taxi About Town
The Rugged Off-roader**